DAVID MORTIMORE BAXTER

Haunted

by KAREN TAYLEUR

illustrated by Brann Garvey

Librarian Reviewer
Laurie K. Holland
Media Specialist (National Board Certified), Edina, MN
MA in Elementary Education, Minnesota State University, Mankato

Reading Consultant
Elizabeth Stedem
Educator/Consultant, Colorado Springs, CO
MA in Elementary Education, University of Denver, CO

 **STONE ARCH BOOKS**
Minneapolis San Diego

David Mortimore Baxter is published by Stone Arch Books
151 Good Counsel Drive, P.O. Box 669
Mankato, Minnesota 56002
www.stonearchbooks.com

Library of Congress Cataloging-in-Publication Data
Tayleur, Karen.
    Haunted!: The Scary Life of David Mortimore Baxter / by Karen Tayleur;
illustrated by Brann Garvey.
        p. cm. — (David Mortimore Baxter)
    ISBN 978-1-4342-0461-5 (library binding)
    ISBN 978-1-4342-0511-7 (paperback)
    [1. Halloween—Fiction. 2. Humorous stories.] I. Garvey, Brann, ill. II. Title.
PZ7.T21149Hau 2008
[Fic]—dc22   2007030744

Summary: David is used to a weird old man answering the door when he rings
Mr. McCafferty's doorbell. But usually, the weird old man is Mr. McCafferty!
His next-door neighbor has been missing for over a week, and when David
finally gets up the nerve to check Mr. McCafferty's house, a stranger answers
the door. Could it be the legendary Shadow Man, who has haunted the town
since a terrible disaster hundreds of years ago? Halloween is coming, and
David doesn't have much time to find out if his neighbor's house is truly
haunted!

Art Director: Heather Kindseth
Graphic Designer: Kay Fraser

Photo Credits
Delaney Photography, cover

1 2 3 4 5 6 13 12 11 10 09 08

Table of Contents

chapter 1
Project Halloween 5

chapter 2
Feeling Green. 12

chapter 3
The Shadow Man. 18

chapter 4
A Family Tradition. 27

chapter 5
Gran's Sad Tale. 34

chapter 6
A Secret Club Meeting. 42

chapter 7
David and the Stranger 49

chapter 8
The Shadow Man Plan. 55

chapter 9
Trapped 62

chapter 10
Unmasked 70

PROJECT HALLOWEEN

At school, we were getting ready for another **Halloween**. I *wasn't very excited*.

Now don't get me wrong, but there are some things you just grow out of. 𝖧𝖠𝖫𝖫𝖮𝖶𝖤𝖤𝖭 is one of them.

"Don't forget your Halloween projects tomorrow," said **Ms. Stacey**, as she left our classroom for a quick trip to the office.

"Project?" I asked. "Since when did we have a project?"

Rose Thornton, my **most unfavorite person**, grunted loudly. She said, "David Mortimore Baxter, you know we have a Halloween project due tomorrow. **Everyone knows that.**"

"We do?" I said.

"Of course," Rose said. "I handed mine in already. I did a presentation on my computer. I'll be showing it before Halloween."

Bec did her famous eye-roll, the one she always saved for Rose.

"Can't wait," said Joe with a YAWN.

Rose smiled. "Ms. Stacey said it was the best project on Halloween she'd ever seen. She said that maybe I should show it to the teachers at the next teachers' meeting."

"Poor teachers," whispered **Joe.**

Then Jake Davern got out of his seat and **pretended to be a ghost.** Then Luke Firth and Chris Lang joined in and it got really NOISY.

Then Ms. Stacey came back. She said unless it got quiet right now, everyone would have to do math during recess.

Just another day at school.

When I got home from school, I grabbed some cookies and milk. Then I headed for my room.

I put my **"No Brothers Allowed"** sign on the door and got down to work, which meant thinking about Halloween.

My little brother, **Harry**, couldn't wait for
Halloween. He'd been planning his costume for
weeks. Every five minutes he would come into
my room to talk about it.

Even when I pointed to my sign that said "No
Brothers Allowed," he just shrugged. He didn't care.

"So what's the best way to **stick this fake knife
into my body?**" he asked.

"You don't actually stick it into your body," I
explained. "That's the point. It's FAKE."

"Ohhhh," said Harry, his eyes shining. "Cool."

I shook my head. I was getting too old to bother
with dressing up and fake blood and plastic knives.

Joe and Bec and I — the only members of the
Secret Club except for **Ralph**, Bec's pet rat —
had already made our plans for Halloween.

We were going to stay at Bec's place and watch
movies and eat candy. We'd been saving up our
allowances for a while.

"So how does a fake knife work?" Harry asked.

I grabbed some paper and drew a picture. Harry finally understood. Then he grabbed the paper and said, **"You stink."** That was his way of thanking me.

I **PUNCHED** him as he walked by. That was my way of saying "You're welcome." Then I got out a few comics, but I couldn't find anything about Halloween in them.

Then **Mom** came in. She said I needed to **peel vegetables** for dinner but I said I was doing my Halloween project and asked if someone else could do it.

Mom pointed at the comic I was reading. I said it was **RESEARCH**.

"I suggest doing research on the Internet," said Mom. "Or you can **peel some carrots.**"

When I went to use the computer, my sister, Zoe, was already using it.

"What do you want, *Dribbles*? Can't you see I'm busy?" she said. I looked at the screen. Zoe was looking at some kind of fashion website.

"I need the Internet," I said. **"For school."**

"Well, I'm using it," Zoe said.

"Mom," I yelled loudly. "Zoe won't let me use the computer."

There was the **thud thud thud** of Mom coming up the hallway and Zoe closed the window she was looking at.

"Zoe, what are you doing?" demanded Mom.

"I'm using the Internet," said Zoe.

"Is it HOMEWORK?" asked Mom.

"Kind of . . ." Zoe said.

"Well?" asked Mom.

Zoe got up and scowled at me. **My sister**
is scary sometimes.

As she headed out the room, she gave me a
dirty look.

Then Mom said, "Zoe, you can peel the carrots."

Zoe GROANED all the way up the hallway.

Once she was gone, I typed "Halloween History" into the search engine and pressed Enter.

There were about **70 billion entries**, so I just clicked on something that looked a little bit boring. Like something Rose Thornton would choose.

I read that Halloween was first celebrated by the **Celts**, who lived 2,000 years ago. I wondered what a **Celt** was. I thought maybe it was some kind of horse.

I wondered what Bec was going to do for her Halloween project. I wrote down some information from the screen. Then I gave Bec a call.

"Did you finish your project, Bec?" I asked when she answered.

"Yep," said Bec. "I made a huge poster with lots of pictures."

Bec was good at drawing. One day she drew this awesome treasure map that looked like the real thing, but that's another story.

"Maybe I could do a **poster**," I said.

"Cool," said Bec.

"Except I don't have any poster paper."

"Oh," said Bec. "Maybe you could do a computer presentation."

"Like Rose Thornton? **No way!**" I yelled.

We talked about a few other ideas, but then I had to go because it was dinnertime.

Dad usually has good ideas for projects, so I asked him what a Celt was. Dad told me it was something that had to do with *Irish people*.

Then I got **the best idea of all time**.

Rose Thornton thought she was going to **impress** everyone with her Halloween project. But wait until Ms. Stacey saw mine!

FEELING GREEN

The next day I handed in my Halloween project. I gave Ms. Stacey the piece of paper.

"Where's the rest of it?" she asked.

"Ummm, that's it," I said. "Actually, that's not all of it." **I pointed to my head.** "Some of it's up here."

"Well, get it out of there and write it down," said Ms. Stacey, "or **you'll be getting an F.**"

"You won't get the **full impact** until I present it," I said.

"That's fine," said Ms. Stacey. "You can present your project first thing tomorrow." She tapped the sheet. "And I expect to see some more written work from you by then, too."

Then Rose Thornton walked over to Ms. Stacey and handed her a notebook. "These are the notes that go with my presentation, Ms. Stacey," she said SWEETLY. "I'm sorry I couldn't hand them in sooner."

"Thank you, **Rose**," said Ms. Stacey.

Rose went back to her desk. **She stuck her tongue out at me on the way.**

I'll show you, I thought.

"Does your aunt still own a costume store?" I asked Joe.

Joe nodded. "Yep. She still does," he said.

The costume store was called **Guess Who**. His aunt Emily owned it.

Joe used to think he would be an actor when he grew up. He used to dress as different characters all the time, until he *wrecked* one of his aunt's costumes. It had taken him 𝔽𝕆ℝ𝔼𝕍𝔼ℝ to save up enough money to pay her back.

"Do you think you could get me this?" I asked.

I handed Joe a list. He nodded again.

* * *

That night I wrote down the story of the **Shadow Man**.

The Shadow Man was a story Dad told us every Halloween.

The Shadow Man lived in the **shadows**.

He was tall and wore dark clothes. He had a thin, wispy voice that **whispered in the night**.

The story didn't scare me, but Harry still climbed into Mom's lap and hid his face when Dad jumped up in the air at the end of the story. Just like he always did.

"Good one, Dad," Zoe would say. "Now tell us something SCARY."

So I wrote the story of the Shadow Man. I used Dad's story, plus I added my own **special** parts.

By the time I finished, I had written four pages.

Ms. Stacey would have to be happy with that.

The next morning I got to school early, which was probably **the first time ever**.

I met Joe at the front door of the school.

He handed me a large shopping bag.

"It's all there," he said. "Good luck." Then we did our **Secret Club handshake.**

I went to the bathroom to get changed. When the bell rang, I went straight to class.

Some people just stared at me. A few kids LAUGHED.

Rose and her friends walked past my desk, but then stopped and stared. "What are you supposed to be?" asked Rose. "The Incredible Hulk?"

"No, I'm a **leprechaun,**" I told her.

I looked at my costume. I didn't think it looked anything like the **Incredible Hulk.**

I started talking to Joe. Then Ms. Stacey came in, dropped her books on her desk, and asked, "What are you doing, David Baxter?"

"I'm ready for my Halloween presentation, Ms. Stacey," I said.

"Why are you dressed like the Incredible Hulk?" she asked.

"It's part of my presentation," I said. "And I'm not dressed like the Incredible Hulk. I'm dressed like a leprechaun. CLEARLY."

Then I stood in front of the classroom with my notes. I read about how Halloween started with the Celts who came from Ireland.

Then **Jake** raised his hand. "Which island?" he asked.

"**Ireland**, not island," I said.

"Let's just wait until David is done. Then we can ask questions," said Ms. Stacey.

So I read the rest of my **History of Halloween** project. It didn't take very long. Then I turned the page.

"And now I would like to read you a Halloween story. It is called The Shadow Man," I said.

I asked Ms. Stacey if we could close the blinds. She sighed, but she said I could. So I did. The room didn't get totally dark, but it was dim — just the effect I was looking for. It needed to be spooky. But I also had to be able to read.

Some of the girls GIGGLED. I took a small flashlight out of my costume bag so I could read my story.

"The Shadow Man," I repeated.

CHAPTER 3

THE SHADOW MAN

This is the story I told them.

The Shadow Man

by David Mortimore Baxter

This story is from **long, long ago**. Long before Bays Park had streets and schools and electricity. Even before the **21 Flavors Ice Cream Parlor** or the **Bays Park Mega Screen Movie Theater.**

Bays Park wasn't even called Bays Park. It was called Reefton's Edge.

It was a mining town, until they mined everything they could out of the ground. Then it just became a regular town like the one we know today.

"That's not true," interrupted Rose.

Ms. Stacey just told her to be quiet.

Anyway, the town started because of the mining. Then the miners came with their wives. Then they had families.

Soon, other people came, people like butchers and bakers, and farmers to grow food, and people who made clothes, and people who could build houses. Then they made schools for the children and **they even built a video store.**

"Ha!" It was Rose again.

Actually, I'm only joking about the video store. They didn't build a video store at all. But they did build a theater, right in the middle of town.

All kinds of people would travel to Reefton's Edge and perform on stage. They had a different play every week.

The theater building was really big. It had rooms for the actors to stay in. It even had a kitchen for them to cook in, but most actors ate at the famous Miss Delia's Cafe.

Everyone from town would come to the theater if there was something playing. That's because **they didn't have TV in those days,** so there was nothing else to do.

They didn't even have electricity, so even if TV had been invented, it wouldn't work without electricity anyway.

Well, Reefton's Edge was a good town. **A rich town.** There was plenty of work and plenty of food and anyone who came to visit usually stayed. It was a nice place to visit, and an even nicer place to live. Life was good in Reefton's Edge.

Then, one day, a theater group came to perform at the theater. They had come to bring **a special play** to the town of Reefton's Edge. Everyone wanted to see the play. Like I said, *there wasn't much else going on.*

Anyway, it was **October 31st.** The whole town came to see the play.

They were used to Miss Maudy playing the piano for plays, but there was no music in the play that night. Everyone felt let down.

In fact, the play turned out to be really boring. There was no music and no dancing and no magic tricks. There was just a whole lot of talking in strange words that didn't make much sense.

The kids got 𝔹𝕆ℝ𝔼𝔻. A couple of old people went to sleep.

The star of the play was a tall man with a whispery voice. The people at the back of the theater couldn't hear him very well.

Someone finally called out, **"Speak up, man!"** Then a few people laughed.

The actor kept talking, but the audience thought it was funny. Someone said, **"Hey, louder!"**

Another person yelled, "Did you say something?"

And on and on they went. The actor finally stopped talking. Miss Maudy marched down to the piano. She started playing it, and everyone clapped and cheered and the actors walked off stage.

Life would have gone back to normal, but that night the Reefton's Edge Theater **caught on fire.**

Someone must have left something cooking on the stove. Or maybe it was a candle that fell over. Anyway, there was a fire, and everyone got out of the theater alive. Or so they thought.

When the sun came up, they found out that someone was missing. It was the lead actor, the guy who'd been EMBARRASSED on stage the night before.

The theater was rebuilt. But after that, things went bad for the town.

First there was a rock fall in the mine. Then there was a whole year without rain and the crops failed for three years in a row.

On every anniversary of the theater fire, somebody VANISHED off the streets of Reefton's Edge, never to be seen again. It was like the town had been cursed.

Hardly anyone visited Reefton's Edge anymore. Performers who came to the theater complained about the annoying man in the bathrobe who hung around backstage.

They said **the man whispered to them while they were performing.**

They never saw the man's face. They called him the **Shadow Man.**

Then the theater **BURNED** down again. No one bothered to rebuild it. The mine closed. People moved to other towns looking for work.

Miss Maudy, who'd had nightmares ever since the first fire, finally put a headstone in the town's graveyard. It read, **"In Memory of the Whispering Actor, May He Rest in Peace."**

That's when the bad things stopped happening to the town. The town council renamed the town Bays Park, which was pretty strange because it wasn't a park and was nowhere near the ocean.

Life got back to normal. Everyone was happy and more people moved to Bays Park. Soon, everyone forgot about the actor who'd been killed in the theater fire.

But every Halloween, the town of Bays Park —
which is still really *Reefton's Edge* — becomes a
little strange.

The wind *whistles* down the alleys.

Cats and **dogs** won't stay outside at night.

Things move silently in the shadows and under the
cover of darkness.

If you happen to be in Bays Park on Halloween,
stay away from the SHADOWS. And don't be found
alone at night.

Because **the Shadow Man might come
for you!**

During the last words of my story, I put the
flashlight under my chin. It lit my face in a spooky
way and a few people SCREAMED. Then everyone
clapped, except Rose, whose face looked like she'd
been **sucking on a lemon**.

"That was good, David. Very good," said Ms.
Stacey. She seemed a little SURPRISED. "And
you wrote that yourself?"

I thought about it. I did actually write down the story all by myself, so I said, "Yes, Ms. Stacey."

"Very good," Ms. Stacey repeated.

I sat down at my desk and Joe gave me a high five. I'd outdone myself this time.

As the morning went on, the special green makeup on my face started to get tight. After a while, I couldn't smile. I couldn't raise my eyebrows. I could hardly talk. **No wonder the Incredible Hulk could only grunt.**

At recess I raced into the boys' bathroom and scrubbed my face with water, but the green wouldn't come off.

"Paper towels," I muttered from the sink.

Joe grabbed a handful and shoved them at me.

Then **Victor Sneddon** walked in. He stopped when he saw me and laughed his *creepy* laugh.

"Well, look who it is," he said. "It's the **Jolly Green Giant** and his sidekick."

Joe and I slipped out the door. "I'd like to send the **Shadow Man** to him," whispered Joe.

"Yeah, I wouldn't mind if the Shadow Man turned up right now," I whispered back.

Afterward I wished I'd never said that. **But by then it was too late.**

CHAPTER 4

A FAMILY TRADITION

When I got home that day, I went straight to Zoe's room and pointed to my face. She just shook her head, led me to the bathroom, and handed me a bottle and some cotton balls.

"This should do it," she said. "Don't forget behind your ears. And don't leave any green stuff on the sink. **Mom will kill you.**"

It took me *FOREVER* to get off all the makeup.

Then I heard Mom calling me. I went to find her.

She was in the kitchen with a bunch of vegetables. This could not be good.

"Oh, David. I'm wondering if you could go to Mr. McCafferty's and see if he has any ketchup," Mom said. "We're out. I need it to make my **veggie loaf.**"

"Oh, great. Veggie loaf," I said.

Mom thinks that I really like veggie loaf. I think it's because once, my dog, Boris, ate a whole pan of it and I **pretended** that I ate it.

Mom started peeling potatoes and shooed me away. "Hurry up," she said.

"Can't Harry go?" I asked.

I hated going to **Mr. McCafferty's**. I thought he was a creepy old man. His house was old and creaky and full of newspapers.

Joe and I thought that Mr. McCafferty used the newspapers to **wrap dead bodies in**.

Bec thought Mr. McCafferty was just a lonely old man. **But how lonely could you be with a basement full of dead bodies?**

Mom was staring at me. "Are you feeling all right, David?" she asked.

"Um, no," I said. "I feel a little STRANGE."

Mom put her hand on my forehead. "Hmmm. Maybe you should lie down. Tell Harry to come and see me," she added.

Harry had to go to Mr. McCafferty's. He came back without the ketchup. By then I was playing tug of war with Boris in my bedroom.

Harry walked by and I asked, "So how was Mr. McCafferty?"

"Not there," said Harry. "There was no one home."

Then he left. **I didn't think about it that much.**

* * *

The next day was Saturday, which is one of my FAVORITE days of the week.

Bec and Joe came over and we practiced being spies in the park across from Mr. McCafferty's house. That was **pretty boring**, because there was no Mr. McCafferty in sight.

"That's weird," said Bec. "He's always home."

I couldn't talk. I was lying on my belly behind a bush. The grass was tickling my nose and **something was crawling up my neck**.

"Hey, what was that?" said Joe next to me, peering over the bush. "Did you see something?"

"Well, maybe if you **shared** those binoculars, I would," said Bec.

I sat up.

"Hand them over, Joe," I said.

I looked at Mr. McCafferty's house through the binoculars, but there was **nothing to see**.

"Nothing to see," I said.

"The bedroom window," said Joe. "I'm sure I saw something in the bedroom window."

I pointed the binoculars back at the window, but there was nothing there. I thought Joe was making it up.

Then I saw it too. The curtain covering the window MOVED.

For a moment, I thought I saw a hand on the curtain. **Then it was gone.**

"He's in the bedroom looking at us," I said. "WEIRD."

Then Bec grabbed the binoculars from me and looked at the house herself. "You two are **dreaming**," she said after a moment. "There's nobody there. **I'm sick of this.** Can we get some lunch? I'm starving."

We ran back to my place. Bec got there first.

Then she said she won and Joe said he didn't know it was a race. They argued about that for a while. Then they argued about seeing things that were, or were not, really there.

* * *

That afternoon, Mom sent Harry back to Mr. McCafferty's with an invitation for Halloween dinner the next Saturday.

But Harry came back with it. **No one had answered the door**, said Harry. Mr. McCafferty wasn't home.

At dinner that night, Dad asked me if I had my costume ready for Halloween. "There's just one week to go," said Dad. "I hear Harry's all ready."

"Not doing it," I said between mouthfuls of pot roast.

"What do you mean?" said Dad. "It's Halloween. The most exciting time of the year. The time when anything can happen." Then he did this ghostly moan.

Zoe raised an eyebrow at him. Harry giggled.

"I've already got the *pumpkin*," said Mom. "Will you carve it, Thomas?"

"Don't I always?" said Dad. "Do you have the **treats** ready, Cordelia?"

"Don't I always?" said Mom. They smiled at each other.

Holidays always did this to my parents. They got all *mushy and lovey-dovey* and talked about how great it was to be together as a family. I thought it was pretty **embarrassing**.

"I'm going to Bec's house," I said. "We already planned it."

"You mean, can you please go to Bec's house?" said Mom, frowning.

"Can I please go to Bec's house?" I asked.

"But it's Halloween," said Dad sadly.

"I might have a party to go to that night," said **Zoe.** Then she added, "If that's okay."

"But it's Halloween," repeated Dad. "It's a family tradition. **Our family tradition.**"

We munched silently on our pot roast.

Then Zoe asked to be excused from the table because she had homework. Harry asked if Dad could help him find the Halloween lights from the garage.

Mom started clearing the table. I helped her, which usually makes her 𝓗𝓐𝓟𝓟𝓨, but she didn't even crack a smile.

"Great pot roast," I said.

But she just nodded with a sad smile. **I never knew smiles could be sad.**

That night I dreamed about fake knives and pumpkins that were as big as houses and something hiding behind Mr. McCafferty's curtain. And even though I couldn't see what it was, there was one thing I was sure of.

That thing behind the curtains at Mr. McCafferty's house wasn't Mr. McCafferty.

CHAPTER 5

GRAN'S SAD TALE

The next day I walked by Mr. McCafferty's house three times. The first two times, I didn't see anything.

No Mr. McCafferty in the garden. No flashing colors from the TV. The curtains were closed.

On the third time past, I saw **Mr. Figgins,** Mr. McCafferty's grumpy old cat, sitting on the low front fence.

Mr. Figgins and I go way back. Let's just say **I don't like him and he doesn't like me.** I still have a scar on my leg from the last time he clawed me.

Still, when I walked past, Mr. Figgins stood up and followed me along the fence. He MEOWED a couple of times, like a regular cat, so I stopped and carefully patted him. Instead of BITING me, Mr. Figgins actually purred. He nudged me for another pat.

It was strange.

I patted him again. Then I walked back home. At the back door, I turned around.

Mr. Figgins was right behind me.

"Mom!" I yelled out. "Mr. McCafferty's cat is here."

Mom came out and said the cat looked HUNGRY and I should feed it.

She was in the middle of cooking Sunday lunch. Sunday lunch was a **big thing** in our house.

Gran, Joe, and Bec came over, and Mom always made **enough food for forty people.**

"It is strange, isn't it?" I said. "That Mr. McCafferty's cat is **hungry?"**

"Animals are always HUNGRY," said Mom. "Give him some of the leftovers from last night."

When I fed Mr. Figgins, he gobbled the food like he hadn't eaten for a week. Then he walked away without a **thank you meow**.

At lunch, I wanted to talk about how Mr. McCafferty was missing, but **Gran** was talking about HALLOWEEN.

"It's a bunch of nonsense," she was saying. Gran was on her third piece of lasagna.

Harry kicked me but I wouldn't look at him. He was always trying to make me L̄AUGH so I'd get into trouble. Our mom thinks table manners are **really important**.

"But my dad loved Halloween," said Dad.

Gran shook her head. "Your father liked a lot of **silly things**," she said. "Halloween. Baseball. Banana cream pie."

Bec raised her eyebrows at me. I shrugged. If there was one thing I knew for sure, you didn't interrupt Gran when she was on a roll.

The best thing to do was to be invisible, finish your meal, and leave.

"Remember that year you dressed up as a PRINCESS, Thomas?" asked Gran.

"That was Susan, Mother," said Dad. "I was a cowboy."

It was *weird* to think of Dad and Aunt Susan as kids.

"That's right," said **Gran**, nodding.

She took a bite of **lasagna**. Then she looked over at me. "And what ꜱilly coꜱtume are you going to wear this year, David?" she asked me.

"David's not doing Halloween this year," said Harry. "He thinks he's **too old** for it."

"Is that right?" said Gran, staring at me. "You know, your grandfather loved Halloween. **Loved it,**" she repeated.

"But you said—" I began.

"Of course there was none of *that garbage you children eat* today. Remember that story he used to tell, Thomas?" she asked.

Dad nodded. "Of course I do, Mother," he said.

"**The Shadow Man,**" she said.

"That was Grandpa's story?" asked Harry.

"Yes," Gran said. "That was your grandfather's story. Only it wasn't a story. **It was true.**"

"Now, Mother," said Dad. "Don't tell the children things that will scare them."

Zoe rolled her eyes.

Gran held up her hand. **"You think you know everything,"** she said. "You grow up and you get a job and have a family and you think you know everything. But let me tell you, you don't. None of you do."

"Would you like more bread, Mom?" asked Dad.

But Gran **wasn't paying attention**. "You young people think you know everything. **You and your computers and your toasters.**"

"I don't think I know everything!" protested Zoe.

"That's right. You don't," said Gran. **"The Shadow Man."** She nodded her head. "Your grandfather would wake up in the middle of the night screaming his name. But no one ever saw that. And now he's **DEAD.**"

"The Shadow Man's dead?" I asked.

Gran thumped the table. "Your grandfather, David," she said. "The one you were named after. **David Mortimore Baxter.**"

Something sneezed under the table.

We all jumped.

It was **Boris**.

"So the Shadow Man's not dead?" asked Harry.

"Who's to say? He's probably dead, but that
doesn't mean he isn't around. **Is there any dessert,**
Cordelia?" asked Gran suddenly. "Or should I have
another piece of lasagna?"

"Everyone ready for dessert?" Mom
asked brightly.

And that was the end of the Shadow Man story.

* * *

That night I tried to talk to Dad about the
Shadow Man, but he kept changing the subject.
I tried to ask Mom, but she just asked me if I
wanted to clean my room.

Zoe said I was being SILLY worrying
about a dumb old story, but she kept
looking around like she was scared.

During the night, something **crept** into my room.

I was just falling asleep when Boris made a low GROWL. My eyes snapped open and I watched the shadow move toward me.

I wanted to yell, wanted to move, but I was frozen. Then the figure pushed me and mumbled, "Hey, David."

It was Harry, holding his favorite blanket.

"**Nightmare?**" I asked.

He just grunted, then made himself comfortable at the foot of my bed. I spent the rest of the night with my feet squished up under my ears.

In the morning Harry was **gone**. The only thing that proved he'd been there was his blanket.

"The Shadow Man," I said aloud.

It sounded STUPID in the daylight. Like a cartoon character. Or somebody out of a comic.

"Stupid story," I said to Boris, giving him  a little shake. Boris just looked at me with his big brown eyes.

"Stupid story," I said again. Then I gave Boris a hug. He whined again.

I couldn't WAIT for Halloween to be over.

CHAPTER 6

A SECRET CLUB MEETING

The next couple of days at school were just normal,
if you could call our school normal.

Rose Thornton kept saying in a very loud voice
that she couldn't talk about her Halloween
costume. That it was a secret. That nobody
would guess what she would be dressing up as,
and we shouldn't even try.

"Who cares?" said Joe.

"I bet you a million dollars that Rose will dress up
as a pop star," said Bec.

Jake Davern also kept talking about a special
costume that he had, but he didn't want to tell
anyone and spoil the surprise.

"I bet it's a 𝕸𝕺𝕹𝕶𝕰𝖄 costume," said Bec.

I didn't want to take that bet, because she was
probably right. Jake had been dressing up in monkey
costumes for Halloween ever since he was old enough
to walk.

James was going to dress as his favorite wrestling champion, **Smashing Smorgan.**

Chris was going to dress up as his favorite **basketball star.**

Stephanie was going to dress up like Frankenstein.

William was going to dress up as a **racecar** **driver.**

Joshua, who **really liked scary things**, had been working on a costume for a month. He wanted to wear it to school but Ms. Stacey wouldn't let him.

Other people talked about the **fake blood** or wigs they'd bought at Guess Who, the costume store that Joe's aunt owns.

"They're such BABIES," said Bec.

"Yeah," said Joe.

"Yeah," I said.

On Monday after school, I walked past Mr. McCafferty's house. The blinds were closed. The house looked like it was SLEEPING.

I was worried about a few things.

The first thing was that Mr. McCafferty had disappeared. I'm not sure why it was **bugging me** so much, but it was.

I guess I was just used to having Mr. McCafferty in his house. Anything else felt STRANGE.

The **second thing** I was worried about was the Shadow Man. I knew the Shadow Man was **just a story**, but Gran's conversation on Sunday had made me *nervous*.

Dad wouldn't talk to me about the Shadow Man, which was really strange, because he was always saying, "You can come and talk to me about anything, son."

The third thing was — well, *I wasn't sure*, but it had something to do with Halloween and that I wasn't going to be part of it.

I checked again to see if Mr. McCafferty was home. He wasn't. I decided it was time for a Secret Club meeting.

I called Joe and Bec.

I asked Bec to bring **The Book**, which was where she wrote down our meeting notes.

"Is it that SERIOUS ?" she asked.

When I said yes, she said she'd come over in five minutes. Joe agreed to come too.

When they arrived, we went into the pantry, turned on the light, and shut the door behind us. Then we settled down on the floor.

Bec opened **The Book** and wrote something down.

"We didn't start the meeting yet," said Joe. "What are you writing?"

"I'm writing down **who's at the meeting**," said Bec.

"Okay," I said. "I call this meeting of the Secret Club to order. I suppose you're wondering why I have called this meeting."

"Just get to the point, David," said Bec. **She rolled her eyes.**

"All right. I have one word for you. MISSING," I whispered.

I watched Bec write down the word in the book.

"What's missing, David?" asked Joe.

"Who," I said. "**Who is missing?**
That is my question."

Bec wrote down Who is missing?

"Actually, I know who is missing," I said.

Bec frowned and crossed out her last sentence.

"I guess my question is why. **Why are they
missing?**" I said.

"Who?" said Bec, who was trying to write
everything down.

"Mr. McCafferty. I already said that,"
I said.

"Actually, you didn't say that at all, David," said
Bec. "Do you want me to read what you have said so
far?"

"What do you mean he's missing?" said Joe.

"I mean he's not there. Vanished. Disappeared.
Missing," I said.

"Maybe he's on vacation," said Bec.

"Maybe he's on a business trip," said Joe.

"He doesn't go on vacation," I said, "and he's RETIRED, so no business trips. No, something strange is going on. I think we should **Investigate.**"

We talked about how to find out if Mr. McCafferty was home or not. **Bec** said we should call him, but I didn't have his number. Joe said I should just knock on the door and have an excuse ready if he opened it.

"Well, Mom did want him to come to dinner next Saturday night for Halloween," I said.

"Great excuse," said Joe. "Hey, Mr. McCafferty is old, isn't he? *Maybe he's met the Shadow Man!*"

"Don't be ridiculous," said Bec.

Then the pantry doorknob rattled. We jumped as the door swung open.

"**Sugar**," said Mom.

Joe handed Mom the sugar bowl. She closed the door again.

"Okay, so someone should knock on his door tomorrow night," I said.

"**You**," said Joe.

"Yep, you," said Bec. "Our plan only makes sense if YOU do it."

"Okay. But you two have to be my backup. Just in case," I said.

They nodded and didn't ask in case of what.

CHAPTER 7

DAVID AND THE STRANGER

The next day, Bec and Joe came home with me after school. They waited in the garage while I walked slowly to Mr. McCafferty's house.

"Hey, Mr. McCafferty," I said under my breath. "Hello, Mr. McCafferty, it's me, David."

I tried out a few more opening lines. Then I was at his door. I raised my fist to knock on the door, but before I could, **the door** CREAKED **open**.

It didn't open far, just wide enough for me to see inside the house. **Whoever opened the door wasn't Mr. McCafferty.**

"What do you want?" asked the creaky old voice from the doorway.

It was a man. I was pretty sure of that. He didn't sound very FRIENDLY. Maybe he thought I was looking for Halloween candy a couple of days too early.

"Is Mr. McCafferty home?" I asked.

But I already knew the answer. **We both did.**

The person who answered the door had done something with Mr. McCafferty. I just knew it. I could feel it in my bones. It was up to me to find out what had happened to Mr. McCafferty.

"He's not here." The voice floated through the open doorway.

I could barely see a **shadowy, tall body**. It was slightly **hunched over** and wearing a bathrobe.

"Can I wait until he gets back?" I asked.

This was part of the plan that Bec and Joe and I had made. I had to get into the house and take a look around. I had to check for signs of a STRUGGLE. Or anything that didn't look quite right.

"He's not coming back for a while. He's on vacation." The voice was **whispery** and **cracked** and **sounded like it came from the bottom of a deep hole.** Not that I'd ever heard a voice from the bottom of a deep hole, but you know what I mean.

"Vacation?" I asked. "Wow, that's really strange. "See, Mr. McCafferty never mentioned going on vacation. I usually feed his cat when he goes away."

Of course, this was **completely untrue**. I never took care of Mr. Figgins, Mr. McCafferty's mean old cat, because Mr. McCafferty never went on vacation. He hardly ever left his house.

I heard the telephone ⓇⒾ𝔑𝔾 inside Mr. McCafferty's house, but the stranger didn't move to answer it.

"That's the phone," I said.

"Yup," he said.

We listened to the phone ring some more. Finally it stopped.

"So," I said, "when's he coming back?"

"I don't know," said the voice. "Maybe this week. Maybe next."

I wanted to ask who he was and what he was doing in Mr. McCafferty's house. Of course, I didn't. **The words wouldn't come out.**

The phone RANG again. I had the crazy idea that it was Mr. McCafferty telling me where he was.

"Rescue me," he would say if I could answer the phone. "Rescue me, **you good-for-nothing boy**."

Mr. McCafferty and I had **never liked each other** much. But just the thought of some stranger messing with my neighbor made me SHIVER. What if he came for me next?

It was a warm day, but a cool breeze blew through the doorway and curled around my legs.

"Well, could you tell me where he is?" I asked. "Because there's something I need to ask him."

"Not sure," said the man. "Maybe I could tell him for you when he calls next."

I shook my head. "No. It's *personal*," I said.

Then the phone rang again. The man said, "I have to go."

He pushed the door shut, but I didn't hear him lock it. I heard him shuffle up the hallway. I could push the door open quickly and slip inside, but what if he caught me?

What if the man with the creaky voice saw me and took me down to the basement and **locked me in there for good?**

I jumped down the two steps that led to Mr. McCafferty's front door. I ran down his sidewalk and jumped over his low fence. Then I felt something grab my shirt.

My life flashed before my eyes. It was a very quick flash.

I turned to face whatever had grabbed me, but it was only one of Mr. McCafferty's **old rose bushes**. I unhooked myself and ran all the way back home. I didn't stop until I reached our garage.

Then I looked around, gave the **Secret Club birdcall**, and waited for the door to open. Bec and Joe were inside. They'd been waiting for me.

"Well?" said Bec.

"Well?" said Joe.

"He's GONE," I said. "Mr. McCafferty's gone."

"What do you mean?" asked Bec.

"Did you see anyone?" asked Joe.

I nodded. I couldn't catch my breath. My heart was 𝒯𝐻𝒰𝓜𝒫𝐼𝒩𝒢 in my chest.

"Well, who?" said Joe. "Who did you see, David? Was it a monster? Was it a creature with slime and huge teeth?"

"Joe!" said Bec, giving him a push.

I shook my head. It was much worse than a **monster** or a **creature**.

"Shadow Man," I said. "I saw the Shadow Man."

CHAPTER 8

By the time I'd told Bec and Joe about my visit to Mr. McCafferty's for the third time, Joe looked scared and Bec looked annoyed.

"Listen," she said, "I think that he did something to Mr. McCafferty. This might be more than we can handle. Maybe we should tell the POLICE."

"Tell them what?" I said. "That the Shadow Man has done something to Mr. McCafferty? Right, I'm sure they'd believe that." **I rolled my eyes.**

"Well, tell your mom," said Joe.

I laughed. "Knowing my mom, she'd invite the Shadow Man over for dinner," I told them. "And then where would we be?"

"Well, what then?" asked Bec.

"We need to get into that house," I said. "And I think I know of a way we can get in. But it will mean dressing up on Halloween. Are you prepared to do that?"

Joe suddenly looked happier than he had for a week. "Well, *only if we have to*," he said.

Bec agreed too. She said she would dress as a 𝙿𝙸𝚁𝙰𝚃𝙴 and Ralph, her rat, could sit on her shoulder.

"There's supposed to be a parrot on your shoulder, not a rat," said Joe.

But Bec said **rats were better than parrots** any day. Then Joe said at least parrots could talk and he'd never heard Ralph say one word. Then I had to stop them before things got really 𝙼𝙴𝚂𝚂𝚈.

I still had some green face paint left over from my Halloween project, so I said I'd dress up as the Incredible Hulk. That way, the Shadow Man wouldn't know who I was if he caught me going through Mr. McCafferty's back door.

Bec said that wasn't a great choice because **I didn't really have any muscles**. I said actually I had more muscles than she did. Then Bec wanted to **arm-wrestle** to prove that she was stronger than me. So I said I didn't need to prove anything but I would agree to arm-wrestle her anyway.

Before we could do that, Joe said that maybe there was an **Incredible Hulk** costume at his aunt's costume store.

"There was one when I picked up your **leprechaun** costume, anyway. Can I use your  phone?" he asked. "I'll call her now."

When he got off the phone Joe said his aunt had just sold an Incredible Hulk costume and **I was lucky** because there was still one left. She would lend me the costume if I would clean the store's windows.

"**Deal**," I said. "What are you going to wear, Joe?"

Joe wasn't sure, but I could tell he was **really excited** to be joining in the Halloween fun.

Then we talked about who would do what, what equipment we should take, and **a back-up plan** in case one of us was caught.

* * *

The next couple of days were **BORING**. I just wanted it to be Halloween. Instead, the next day we had to sit through Rose's **boring** presentation of Halloween.

It was just a slideshow of pictures of her dressed up in different Halloween costumes. "That's me when I was three," explained Rose. "As you can see, I am dressed up here as a **fairy princess**."

It went on and on.

William's presentation about Halloween cars was pretty interesting and Kate's project on Halloween music from movies was SPOOKY.

On Friday after school, Joe brought over my Halloween costume. **Mom** answered the door, so I had to explain to her that I was going to join in the family Halloween fun after all.

I felt mean when she gave me a huge hug and said, *"Fantastic."* I wanted to tell her what we were up to.

"Does that mean you and Joe will join us for dinner on Saturday night?" asked Mom.

"And Bec," I said.

Meanwhile, Joe was in the living room, looking at the decorations that Dad and Harry had hung up.

"This is COOL," said Joe. "Are those new lights?"

A long string of pumpkin lights were hung across the window. They were partly covered by fake cobwebs and a huge black rubber spider.

There was another string of lights outside decorating the roof. And there were more spiders on the back door. There were pictures of pumpkins and spiderwebs all over the place. Dad had bought out the entire Halloween section at the supermarket and everything was hanging up in our house.

When Dad decorates for Halloween, **he decorates everything**. He even tried to decorate Zoe's room, but everything in there is black and creepy anyway.

"Yes, the lights are new," Mom said. "*Harry wants to dress Boris up* for trick or treating. David's father and Harry have been carving the pumpkin. Those two have gone *overboard* this year."

Joe and I went into my room and shut the door and talked about our plan again. We ran through the steps to make sure we knew EXACTLY what was supposed to happen.

Shadow Man Plan

1. Dress in Halloween costumes.

2. Bec and Joe and David go to Mr. McCafferty's house.

3. Bec and Joe go to front door, trick or treating. If Mr. McCafferty answers the door, end of plan. Everything okay. If not, go to step 4.

4. David goes around to back door to go inside. He will have a flashlight, for emergencies only. Bec and Joe keep Shadow Man busy while David looks around. Make sure to check the basement.

5. David takes photos inside house with Zoe's digital camera. If possible, he will take a photo of Shadow Man before leaving the house.

6. Go back home and call police.

7. Have dinner with family.

Joe and I agreed that it was **a pretty good plan.** Then we walked past Mr. McCafferty's house once or twice, just to make sure that he wasn't back.

On the second time past, I thought I saw a curtain move, but **I probably just imagined it.**

Then Joe went home and I went to bed early. *Tomorrow was going to be a big day.*

It was kind of EXCITING and kind of **scary.** By bedtime the next night, we would know the truth about Mr. McCafferty. We would know **the truth** about the Shadow Man.

The thing is, I didn't think I was ready for **the truth**.

CHAPTER 9

TRAPPED

The next day, I was getting a little nervous, so I got ready early.

I tried on my costume. I had to get Zoe to zip it up because the zipper was on the back and I couldn't reach it. Then Zoe put my green makeup all over my face.

Then I watched a *spooky* DVD with Harry and Dad. They were getting into the Halloween *mood*.

Halfway through the movie, Mom brought in some popcorn. **Harry had to throw the popcorn into my mouth** because I had my rubber Hulk hands on.

At five o'clock, Bec came over. She was wearing her **pirate costume**, but she didn't have Ralph the rat with her.

"Mom wouldn't let me bring him," she explained. **"You look green,"** she added.

Then Joe came over. He was wearing a bathrobe.

"Oh," said Bec. "Don't tell me. You're **a person who's about to take a bath.**"

Joe shook his head. "You know who I am," he said in a *whispery, spidery voice* that sent shivers through my green skin.

"The Shadow Man," I said.

Joe nodded. "Yup."

Then Mom told us that we had to line up in front of the fireplace. She wanted to take a picture.

Harry was already there. He had a **fake knife** sticking out of his arm and **fake blood** oozing from his **fake wound.**

"Mom wouldn't let me put the knife on my head," he grumbled. "She said it was **too gross.**"

Gran, who was there for dinner, looked at all of us. She frowned at me. **She rolled her eyes at Harry.** She raised her eyebrows when Joe told her who he was.

Then Zoe, wearing her usual black clothes, came into the room to look at us.

Gran clapped her hands. "Now, that's a good costume!" she said. "What are you?"

Zoe just stared at her. "I'm not wearing a costume," she said.

Then Dad brought the carved pumpkin in. Everybody said it looked **great**, even though the face looked pretty CROOKED, if you asked me.

Mom said that **Boris** was not allowed to go trick or treating with Harry. Harry looked like he was going to cry.

When Joe and Bec and I headed out the door, Mom pushed Harry with us. "Have fun," she said.

"Harry's not coming with us," I said.

"Yes, he is," said Mom. "He's old enough to go with you. I want you to take care of him, David. **Be a good big brother.**"

"He'll WRECK everything!" I yelled.

I couldn't believe it. Mom was WRECKING our plan and it was all **Harry's fault**.

"Do what your mother says," said Dad.

"You have an hour before dinner's ready," warned Mom.

Already the light outside had turned GLOOMY. I walked past Gran to get to the front door. She stopped me with her walking stick and looked me in the eye.

"Be careful out there, David," she warned quietly. **"Remember."** That's all she said, but I knew what she meant.

Out on the street, Bec and Joe were arguing about what to do with Harry.

"We can't take him with us," said Joe. "It's too RISKY."

"What's too risky?" asked Harry.

"Well, we can't leave him **alone**," said Bec.

We finally agreed that Harry could come along. But he had to do exactly what we told him.

"Don't say anything," I warned.

"Can I say **trick or treat**?" asked Harry.

"Yes. But that's all," I said.

We were in front of Mr. McCafferty's house. I grabbed Harry by the shoulders and bent down to whisper in his ear.

"Don't do anything, okay?" I told him. "Just say trick or treat. Nothing else. Just stand at the door. Unless Joe or Bec tells you to run. Then you run. Do you hear me? **You run as fast as you can.**"

Harry's eyes were wide and he nodded quickly. I guess my Hulk muscles must have SCARED him, even though they were fake.

As Bec and Joe and Harry walked up Mr. McCafferty's sidewalk, I noticed a group of people coming my way.

"Trick or treat!" they yelled.

Oh, no. It was **Rose Thornton** and her friends.

"Oooh, look who it is," sang out Rose. "A big bad **leprechaun**."

"I'm the Incredible Hulk," I said angrily. I rubbed my face.

The makeup was starting to get tight. I shouldn't have put it on so early. It was making my nose itch and making my lips stretch into a smile. And I needed to go to the bathroom, which was bad timing.

Rose was dressed up like a rock star. She was wobbling around on some really high shoes. Her blond wig was slipping off to one side, which made her look WEIRD.

"You can't be here," I said. "We're already here."

"Fine," Rose said, tossing her head. "We'll go to the next house. Come on, girls."

I watched them move on to the next house. Then I quickly walked around to the back of Mr. McCafferty's house.

Just as I reached the back door, I heard the thud of someone BANGING on the front door. I waited.

Then I heard Harry yell **"Trick or treat!"** when somebody opened the door.

I took a deep breath. I checked inside my bag once more, which was hard to do with my **large rubber hands.**

The flashlight and camera were both there. I carefully turned the doorknob and pushed at the door. It opened easily and **I poked my head in** to make sure no one was around.

I could hear talking from the front door.

I quickly slipped inside and headed for Mr. McCafferty's bedroom. I was expecting to see him **tied up** inside, but there was no one there.

Next I looked in the bathroom, but no one was there either. I could still hear voices at the door, so I scooted to the basement door and went down the stairs.

It was pretty dark, so I pulled out my flashlight and turned it on. *The light made creepy shadows on the wall.* I kept expecting something to jump out and grab me. But there was nothing there.

No MONSTERS.

No **dead bodies** wrapped in newspaper.

No Mr. McCafferty.

Just then, I heard the front door slam. Then I heard footsteps walking in the hallway above my head.

I switched off the flashlight and stopped breathing, just in case the Shadow Man had incredible hearing powers.

The door to the basement, which I'd left open a little, suddenly slammed shut.

I was trapped.

CHAPTER 10

UNMASKED

After a minute, I started breathing again. I wasn't sure what to do.

I couldn't believe that Joe and Bec had left me in the basement to die. I tried to figure out what they would do.

Would they call the police?

Would they go to my house and *tell Mom and Dad?*

Maybe the Shadow Man had already **captured** them and he was wrapping them up in newspaper.

What about Harry? If anything happened to him, *my parents would kill me.*

The makeup on my skin was really tight now. I tried to *whisper* something but my lips wouldn't move properly.

Instead of saying "Joe" I could only say, "Oh."

Things were very, very bad.

Plus, I still had to go to the bathroom. I tried not to think about the last **three cups of juice** I'd had before leaving my house. I tried to get out of my costume but I couldn't reach the ZIPPER. Even if there was a bathroom nearby, I couldn't have used it because I was stuck in the suit.

I climbed the stairs to the basement door and tried turning the knob, but the door was locked from the outside. So I went back down into the basement and looked around for somewhere to sit. There was a pile of newspapers, so I sat down on them and waited.

I heard footsteps upstairs. I knew it was the Shadow Man. **He'd just been waiting for us to make a wrong move!**

I hid in the shadow of the stairs. The footsteps moved to the basement door and the knob rattled. Then the door opened.

A blast of light shone down the stairs. I huddled deeper in the shadows.

"Hello?" said **a thin, creaky voice.** "Is someone down here?"

I heard a KNOCK on the front door. The Shadow Man didn't move. I held my breath. Then there was another knock at the door and I heard him sigh.

He closed the door and I breathed again.

"Trick or treat," I heard someone say.

I was halfway out from under the stairs when the door swung open fully and a light shone straight in my face.

I was dead.

I tried to scream, but my lips were stuck in a straight line. "Uhhhh. Uhhhhh," was all I could say.

"Yes, you're the Incredible Hulk, very good." It was Bec. "Now, come on. We don't have all day."

I tiptoed up the stairs toward the light. Then Bec pushed me and whispered, "RUN!"

We ran down the hallway and out the back door. It slammed behind me, but I didn't care.

As we ran around the corner, I saw Rose and her friends standing at the front door looking very surprised.

A thin, old hand reached out from the front door. **The hand pointed our way**, but Bec and I just kept running. We didn't stop until we got home.

Joe and Harry were waiting for us in the garage.

"Did you get any **pictures**?" said Joe.

I hadn't used the camera at all.

I made Joe unzip my costume. **Then I ran inside, straight to the bathroom.**

In the bathroom, I did what I had to do. Then I used a whole bottle of Zoe's makeup-removing lotion to get rid of my green skin. It took me **forever**.

Finally, Mom came to the door and asked if I was going to join everyone for dinner or not.

I didn't know what to do. I didn't want to have dinner. I needed to talk to Bec and Joe and figure out what we should do next. Obviously the Shadow Man had gotten rid of **Mr. McCafferty's body.** Then he'd seen us running away, so we were next on the list.

After I changed into some normal clothes, I sat down at the dinner table.

Joe and Bec had changed out of their costumes. They kept looking at me.

Zoe must have decided not to go to her party, because she was sitting next to Dad. Harry was really quiet.

"How did you do?" asked Dad loudly.

I jumped. "What?" I asked.

"How many treats did you get?" he asked.

"Oh, not many," I said.

When the doorbell rang **I jumped again**.

Mom got up to answer the door. "That must be our guest," she said.

"Guest?" I ECHOED.

"Hello," said a thin, creaky voice. **It was a voice I'd know anywhere.**

I looked up and saw an incredibly old, tall, thin man standing next to my mother.

It was the Shadow Man.

He was here to take me away!

I opened my mouth, but nothing came out.

"This is **Mr. Fitzgerald**," said Mom.
"He's Mr. McCafferty's cousin. He's been taking
care of Mr. McCafferty's house."

"I bet," I mumbled.

"What, David?" asked Mom.

"I said . . . um . . . where is Mr. McCafferty? Where
is he?" I demanded.

"Mr. McCafferty is at a Rose Growers' Convention,"
said Mom. "Apparently, he gave you a letter to tell
me what was going on." Mom was looking at me,
frowning.

"A letter?" I said slowly. A weird feeling began in
my stomach, **like my insides were sliding into a
hole.** "A letter?" I repeated.

Suddenly, I REMEMBERED.

About a week ago, Mr. McCafferty had shoved a **letter** at me as I ran past his house. "Give this to your mother," he'd said.

I'd taken the letter, but Mom wasn't home.

The last thing I remembered was putting the letter on top of the fridge. That's the last time I even thought about it.

"Oh," I said.

Mom said, "Please sit down, Mr. Fitzgerald. I'm so sorry about the **mix-up**. I'm glad I came over yesterday to ask Mr. McCafferty to dinner. I'm so happy you could make it instead!"

And then Mom introduced the Shadow Man — I mean Mr. Fitzgerald — to everyone at the dinner table. Gran stared at him and then nodded. Bec and Joe looked relieved.

I wondered if Mr. Fitzgerald had told Mom about my visit the other day. He looked at me once — **a long look** — but then he kept on eating.

Around dessert time, he told us that some children had been **up to no good** around his back door, but he only caught a glimpse of them as they ran off.

Mom looked 𝕊ℍ𝕆ℂ𝕂𝔼𝔻 and said she was sure they meant no harm.

Then the doorbell rang again.

Dad answered it to a chorus of "trick or treat."

There, standing at the door, was the Incredible Hulk. (Of course, it wasn't the real Incredible Hulk. It was someone dressed up.)

"Hi Zoe," said the Hulk.

When the Hulk took off his mask, we could see that it was **Victor Sneddon**, the school bully. He really liked my sister, Zoe.

"That's him," said Mr. Fitzgerald, pointing to Victor. "He tried to steal from me. **Grab him, grab him,**" he said in his whispery, thin voice.

"I'll call the police," Harry said.

"Grab him," insisted Mr. Fitzgerald, as Victor stood at the door with his treat bag open.

It took a long time for everything to settle down.

We **finally** convinced Mr. Fitzgerald that it must have been another person in an Incredible Hulk costume that he had seen RUNNING away from the house. He wasn't sure he believed us, but he didn't really have a choice.

I gave Victor some candy. He shook his head and said I had a **weird family**.

Then Mom served dessert and Dad told us the **Shadow Man** story because that was our tradition on Halloween night. When Dad JUMPED in the air at the end of the story, Mr. Fitzgerald jumped too.

Gran just laughed. "I love that story," she said, wiping her eyes.

"But Gran, you said that was **a true story**," said Zoe.

"**RIDICULOUS**. It's just a silly story, that's all," said Gran, helping herself to another piece of pie.

After a couple more hours, Bec and Joe finally went home and Mr. Fitzgerald left too.

Harry said it was **the best Halloween ever.**

Then Dad carried him to bed.

Gran got ready to leave. She asked me to help her out to her car with some leftovers.

As I slipped a piece of wrapped pie onto Gran's back seat, something grabbed my shoulder.

It was Gran.

"**He's real, you know,**" she whispered into my ear. "**The Shadow Man is real.**"

A **cold wind** whipped around my ankles.

Then Gran laughed.

I watched her drive off into the night. Then I ran inside and slammed the front door behind me.

Of course, I knew she was joking.

Then I **locked** the door.

Just in case.

The End

About the Author

When Karen Tayleur was growing up, her father told her many stories about his own childhood. These stories continued to grow. She says, "I always enjoyed the retelling, and wanted to create a character who had the same abilities with 'bending the truth.'" And David Mortimore Baxter was born! Karen lives in Australia with her husband, two children, two cats, and one dog.

About the Illustrator

Brann Garvey grew up in the great state of Iowa, where he studied art and visual communications. He graduated from the Minneapolis College of Art & Design with a degree in illustration. Brann is usually found with one or more of the following: a pencil in his hand, a comic book, a remote for watching DVDs, or his pet kitty, Iggy. When the weather is nice, Brann likes to play disc golf, and he proudly points out that Iowa is one of the world's centers for the sport. Iggy does not play.

Glossary

binoculars (buh-NOK-yuh-lurz)—an instrument that you look through with both eyes to make distant things seem closer

Celts (KELTS)—a group of people who lived in Europe two thousand years ago

creaky (CREEK-ee)—squeaky or rusty-sounding

impact (IM-pakt)—the effect something has on a person

investigate (in-VESS-tuh-gate)—to find out as much as possible about something

leprechaun (LEP-ruh-kon)—a small, lucky sprite from Irish folklore

notes (NOHTS)—words written down to record things that happen during a meeting

presentation (pree-zen-TAY-shuhn)—a special report someone makes in front of a group of people

project (PROJ-ekt)—a school assignment

tradition (truh-DISH-uhn)—something that a group of people does every year

Discussion Questions

1. Does your family have any traditions for holidays or other special days? What are they? Talk about different traditions.

2. At the end of this book, Gran tells David that the Shadow Man story is true. What do you think?

3. David has to prepare a presentation about Halloween. Some people get very nervous about doing presentations. What are some things that you can do to make the presentation seem less scary?

Writing Prompts

1. Every year, David's father tells the story of the Shadow Man. Do you know any scary stories? Write one down, remembering to be descriptive. Draw a picture to go along with it if it will help the story.

2. David doesn't get along with Mr. McCafferty, but he's worried when his neighbor seems to have disappeared. Do you have neighbors? Describe them, and write about your relationship with them.

3. David dresses up like a leprechaun, but everyone thinks he's the Incredible Hulk! What costume would you like to wear? Describe it, and draw a picture!

David Mortimore Baxter

David is a great kid, but he has one big problem — he can't stop talking. These wildly humorous stories, told by David himself, will show readers just how much trouble a boy and his mouth can get into, whether he's going on a class trip, trying to find a missing neighbor, running a detective agency, or getting lost in the wild. David is amiable, engaging, cool, and smart enough to realize that growing up is the biggest adventure of all.

Internet Sites

Do you want to know more about subjects related to this book? Or are you interested in learning about other topics? Then check out FactHound, a fun, easy way to find Internet sites.

Our investigative staff has already sniffed out great sites for you!

Here's how to use FactHound:

1. Visit *www.facthound.com*

2. Select your grade level.

3. To learn more about subjects related to this book, type in the book's ISBN number: **9781434204615**.

4. Click the **Fetch It** button.

FactHound will fetch the best Internet sites for you!